My Bibi Always Remembers

by Toni Buzzeo

Illustrated by Mike Wohnoutka

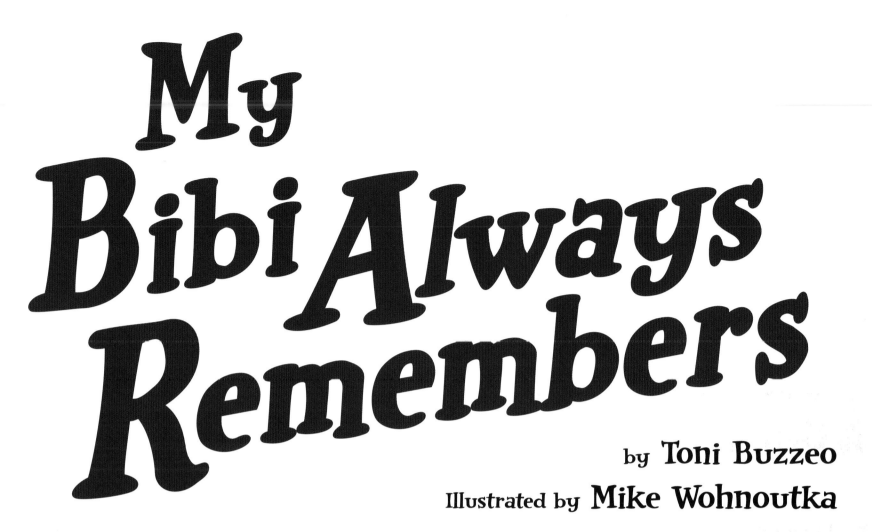

DISNEY · HYPERION BOOKS

NEW YORK

In memory of my beloved Gram, Mae Mackey. I will always remember you.
—T.B.

In memory of Grandma Malecek and Grandma Wohnoutka
—M.W.

Text copyright © 2014 by Toni Buzzeo
Illustrations copyright © 2014 by Mike Wohnoutka

First Edition
10 9 8 7 6 5 4 3 2 1
H106-9333-5-14135
Printed in Malaysia
Reinforced binding
Designed by Michelle Gengaro-Kokmen

Library of Congress Cataloging-in-Publication Data

Buzzeo, Toni.
My Bibi always remembers / by Toni Buzzeo ; illustrated by Mike Wohnoutka.—First edition.
pages cm
Summary: Tembo, a little African elephant, wants to be just like her grandmother, Bibi, but is often distracted when
she is supposed to be following Bibi to a watering hole. Includes a note about elephants.
ISBN 978-1-4231-8385-3
[1. African elephant—Fiction. 2. Elephants—Fiction. 3. Animals—Infancy—Fiction.] I. Wohnoutka, Mike, illustrator.
II. Title.
PZ7.B9832My 2015
[E]—dc23   2013007146

Visit www.DisneyBooks.com

In Swahili, **Bibi** is the word for Grandmother,
and **Tembo** is the word for Elephant.
Elephants communicate across distances with a long, low rumble.

RUMMMMBLE!

Thirsty little Tembo hears her Bibi across the wide, parched plain.

When Bibi calls,
everyone comes—
aunties, sisters, Mama—
one by one.
Step-step.
Searching for wet.

But Tembo has a better idea!
She remembers playing jackalberry tag with Mama.
Tembo chews a mouthful of dark green leaves,
then pokes her trunk into the jackalberry tree,
searching for drops of dew.

When Tembo looks up, she is all alone.
Wind whistles through the acacia trees.
Tembo squeals.

Which way should I go?

She waits and listens.

Through the tall brown grass,
Mama's soft steps vibrate.
She wraps Tembo with her long, gray trunk.
   Come along, Little Tembo.
   Bibi remembers the way.

RUMMMMBLE!

When Bibi calls,
everyone comes—
one by one.
Step-step.
Searching for wet.

But Tembo has a better idea!
She remembers playing stork chase with Auntie.
Stork taunts,
    all flapping wings and bossy squawk.
Tembo chases,
    all flapping ears and tiny trumpet.

When Tembo looks up, she is all alone.
Baboons chatter in the heat.
Tembo squeals.
Which way should I go?
She waits and listens.

From ten tails far away,
Auntie appears through the wavering heat.
Her trunk curls around Tembo's round rump.
Come along, Little Tembo.
Bibi remembers the way.

RUMMMMBLE!

When Bibi calls,
everyone comes—
one by one.
Step-step.
Searching for wet.

But Tembo has a better idea!
She remembers hide-and-seek under
Bibi's broad shade.
Her small footsteps
slow,
slip,
stop.
She slides into a small patch of cool
and drifts into a thirsty dream.

When Tembo awakes, she is all alone.
Hyenas laugh near the trees.
Tembo squeals.
Mama, which way should I go?
She waits and listens.

Lions huff in the grass.
Tembo squeals again.
Auntie, which way should I go?
She waits and listens.

Finally, Tembo remembers.
She squeals one last time.
    Bibi, which way should I go?

In the distance comes a rumbling,
closer and closer, until—
Bibi crashes into sight.

She brings Mama and Auntie and all of Tembo's family.
Ears flapping, trunks high, they circle Tembo and trumpet.

BRRRRRRRRRRRRAW!

    Come along, Little Tembo.
    Bibi remembers the way.

As sun sinks low in the west,
Tembo and Bibi turn to follow.
They lead the family around one last bend.
And then—
Bibi stops.
Here is the spot she has always remembered.

BRRRRRRRRRRRRRAW!

Tembo echoes Bibi's call.

brrrrrrrrrrrraw!

Bibi digs in the sandy riverbed
with long, tough tusks.
Tembo digs in the dry sand too
with her stubby milk tusks.
At last, a very small puddle
of very muddy water forms.

Bibi and Tembo dig and dig.
The puddle grows wider and deeper
until stars shine back at the sky.

With her long, strong trunk
Bibi draws up a sip.
She sprays, and the cool water
slides slick down Tembo's throat.

RUMMMMBLE!

When Bibi calls,
everyone comes—
one by one.
Step-step.
To drink the wet.

Bibi strokes Tembo with her long, gray trunk.
Tembo nestles snug against Bibi's side.
Someday I will be the Bibi,
and then I will always remember.

Author's Note

Elephant babies live in families of twelve or more elephants that include mothers, daughters, sisters, aunts. They all care for and protect the babies of the family. The oldest, largest, and most experienced elephant—the grandmother—is the matriarch of the family. It is her job to make decisions for the family and to remember where food and water can be found, even when there is a long drought. Females remain in the family for their whole lives, but young males leave the family to join a bachelor herd when they are about twelve to fifteen years old.

Because African elephants are threatened, the Amboseli Trust for Elephants is dedicated to helping Africa's elephants survive and thrive in their native home. To learn more about their work, visit elephanttrust.org.